Shark Bites

Great White Shark

by Jenna Lee Gleisner

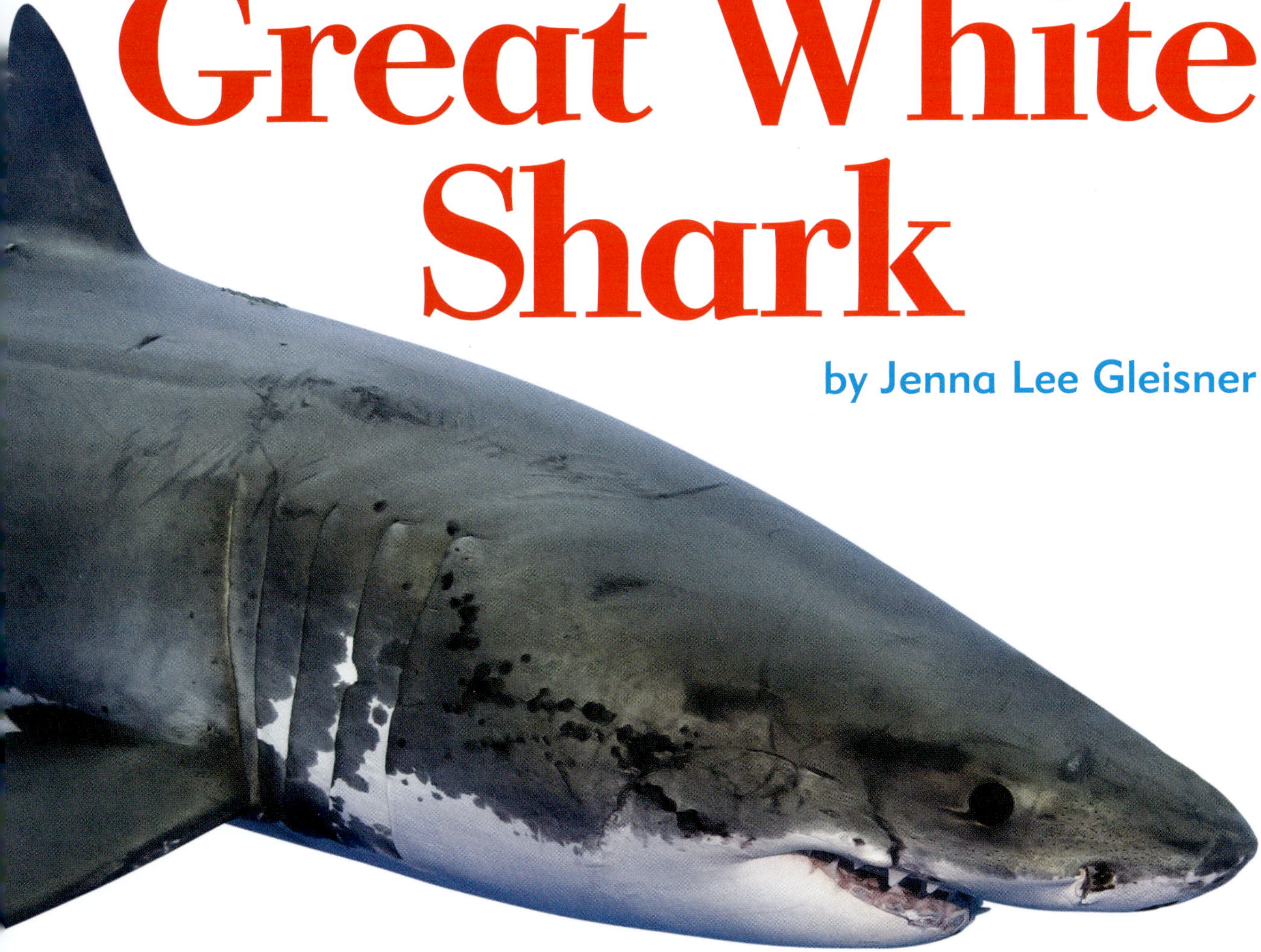

Ideas for Parents and Teachers

Bullfrog Books let children practice reading informational text at the earliest reading levels. Repetition, familiar words, and photo labels support early readers.

Before Reading
- Discuss the cover photo. What does it tell them?
- Look at the picture glossary together. Read and discuss the words.

Read the Book
- "Walk" through the book and look at the photos. Let the child ask questions. Point out the photo labels.
- Read the book to the child, or have him or her read independently.

After Reading
- Prompt the child to think more. Ask: Great white sharks are large and fierce! Have you ever seen one? Would you want to?

Bullfrog Books are published by Jump!
5357 Penn Avenue South
Minneapolis, MN 55419
www.jumplibrary.com

Copyright © 2020 Jump! International copyright reserved in all countries. No part of this book may be reproduced in any form without written permission from the publisher.

Library of Congress Cataloging-in-Publication Data

Names: Gleisner, Jenna Lee, author.
Title: Great white shark / by Jenna Lee Gleisner.
Description: Bullfrog books edition.
Minneapolis, MN : Jump!, Inc., [2020]
Series: Shark bites
Includes bibliographical references and index.
Audience: Age 5-8. | Audience: K to Grade 3.
Identifiers: LCCN 2018060105 (print)
LCCN 2019000029 (ebook)
ISBN 9781641289627 (ebook)
ISBN 9781641289610 (hardcover : alk. paper)
Subjects: LCSH: White shark—Juvenile literature.
Classification: LCC QL638.95.L3 (ebook)
LCC QL638.95.L3 G54 2020 (print)
DDC 597.3/3—dc23
LC record available at https://lccn.loc.gov/2018060105

Editors: Susanne Bushman and Jenna Trnka
Design: Shoreline Publishing Group

Photo Credits: Wildestanimal/Shutterstock, cover, 6–7, 22; VisionDive/Shutterstock, 1; BW Folsom/Shutterstock, 3; Alessandro de Maddalena/Shutterstock, 4, 14; Andrea Wolochow/Shutterstock, 5; Sergey Uryadnikov/Dreamstime, 8–9, 23tr; Sergey Uryadnikov/Shutterstock, 10, 18–19, 23tl, 24; Ramon Carraterro/Shutterstock, 11; CD Ascher/iStock, 12–13, 23bl; Valerijs Novickis/Dreamstime, 15; Natursports/Shutterstock, 16–17; Jeff Rotman/Getty, 20–21; Linda Johnsonbaugh/Dreamstime, 23br.

Printed in the United States of America at Corporate Graphics in North Mankato, Minnesota.

Table of Contents

A Great Hunter 4
Parts of a Great White Shark 22
Picture Glossary 23
Index 24
To Learn More 24

A Great Hunter

What shark has 300 teeth?

dorsal fin

And a fin like this?

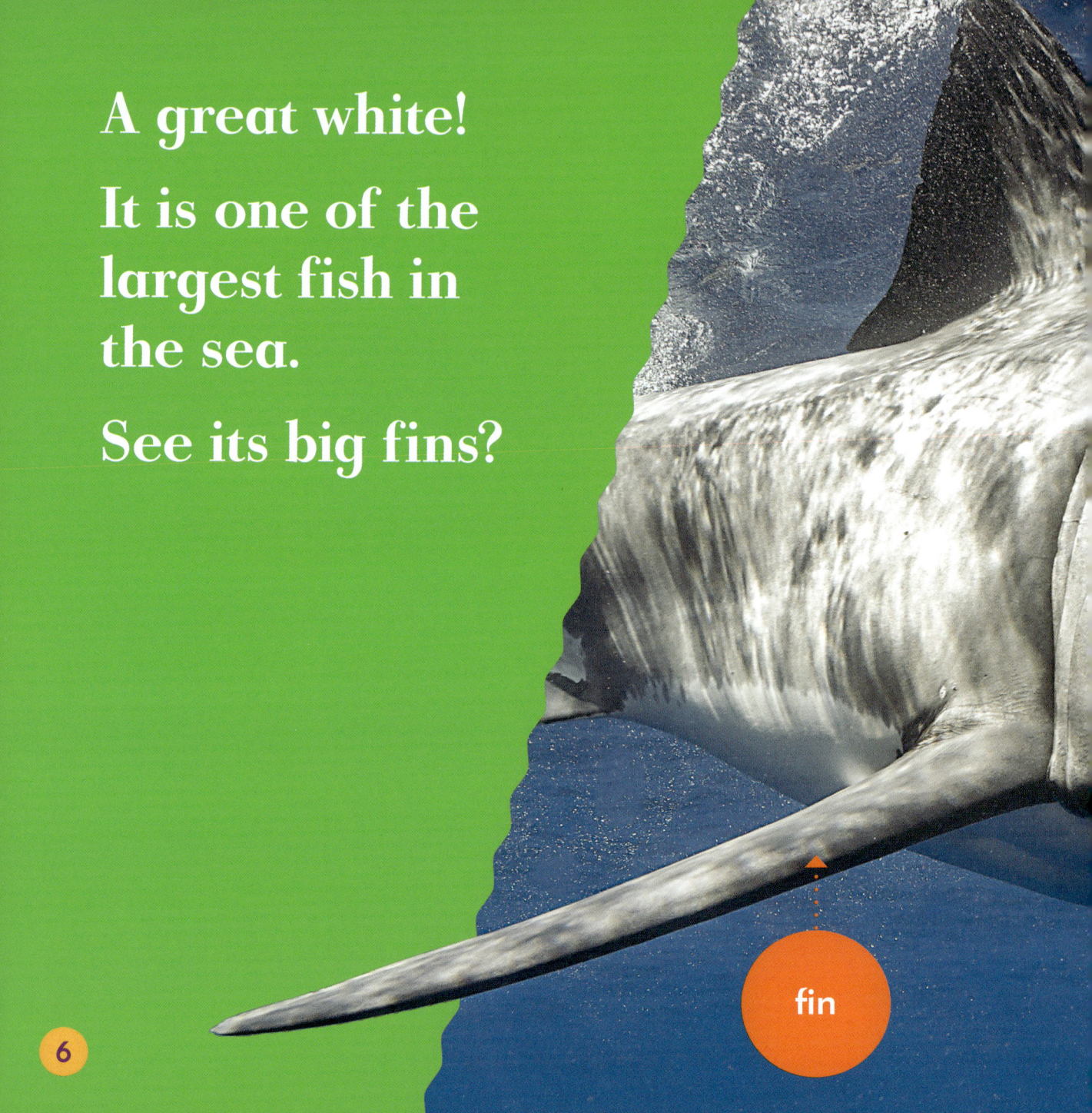

A great white!

It is one of the largest fish in the sea.

See its big fins?

fin

A great white is fierce.

And built to hunt.

Wow!

Its tail is big.
And powerful.

tail

Zoom!

It helps the shark swim fast.

Its snout is pointed.

Its body has a torpedo shape.

Sniff! Sniff!

The great white smells well.

What does it smell?

A seal!
It is two miles (3.2 kilometers) away.

Its body is gray on top.

It blends in
with the water.

Can the seal see it?

No.

Pow!

It breaches!

It takes the seal by surprise.

We want to learn more.

Be safe!

What do you like about great whites?

Parts of a Great White Shark

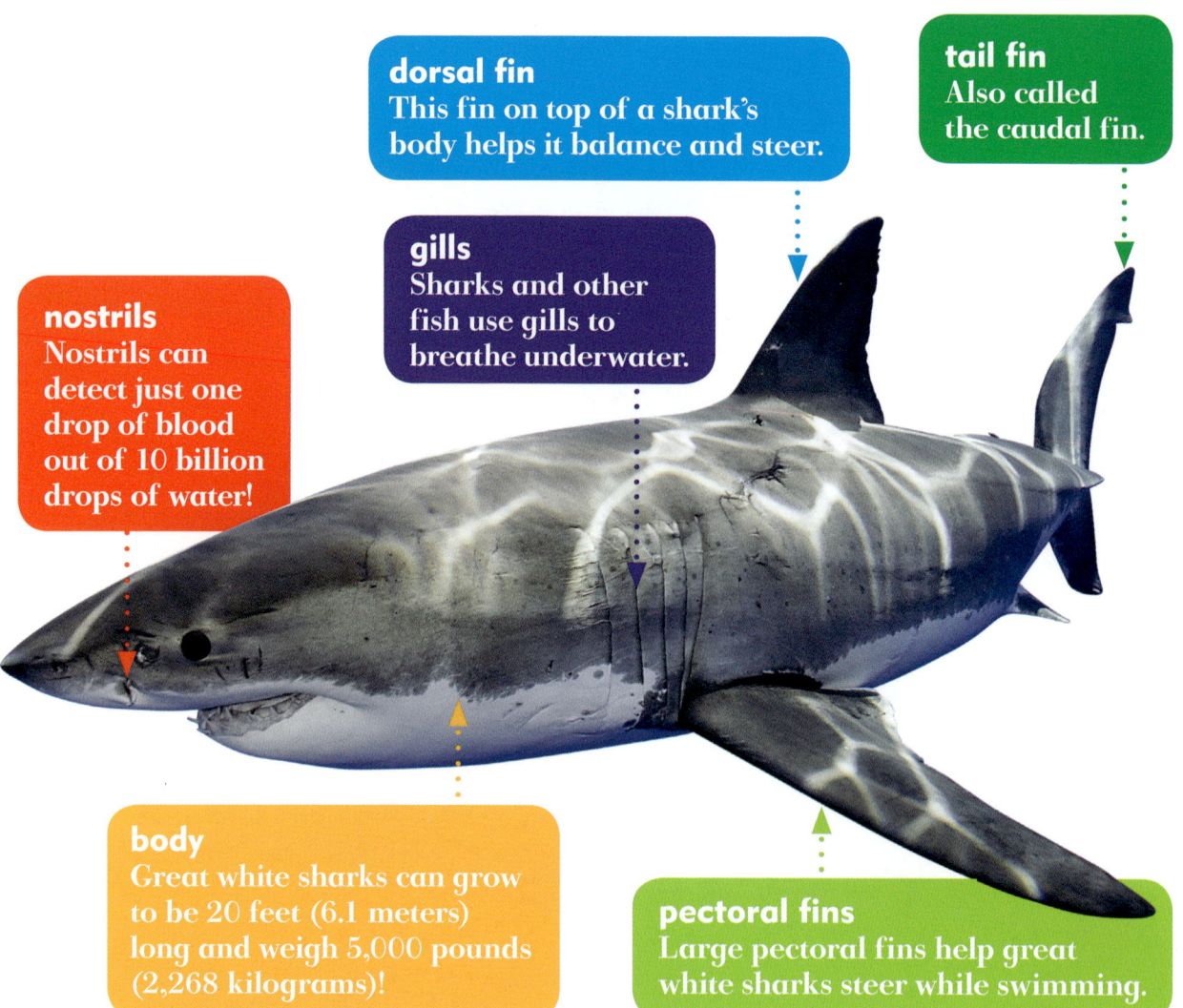

dorsal fin
This fin on top of a shark's body helps it balance and steer.

tail fin
Also called the caudal fin.

gills
Sharks and other fish use gills to breathe underwater.

nostrils
Nostrils can detect just one drop of blood out of 10 billion drops of water!

body
Great white sharks can grow to be 20 feet (6.1 meters) long and weigh 5,000 pounds (2,268 kilograms)!

pectoral fins
Large pectoral fins help great white sharks steer while swimming.

Picture Glossary

breaches
Jumps out of and breaks through the surface of the water.

fierce
Violent or dangerous.

snout
The long front part of an animal's head that includes the nose, mouth, and jaws.

torpedo
A thin, pointed, cylinder-shaped underwater device.

Index

body 12, 17
breaches 18
fierce 9
fin 5, 6
gray 17
hunt 9
seal 15, 17, 18
smells 14
snout 12
swim 11
tail 10
teeth 4

To Learn More

Finding more information is as easy as 1, 2, 3.

❶ Go to www.factsurfer.com

❷ Enter "greatwhiteshark" into the search box.

❸ Choose your book to see a list of websites.